Dilly Dog's Dizzy Dancing

by Barbara deRubertis • illustrated by R.W. Alley

THE KANE PRESS / NEW YORK

Alpha Betty's Class

Dilly Dog

Alexander Anteater

Bobby Baboon

Corky Cub

Hanna Hippo

Eddie Elephant

Frances Frog

Gertie Gorilla

Lana Llama

Izzy Impala

Jeremy Jackrabbit

Kylie Kangaroo

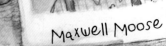
Maxwell Moose

Library of Congress Cataloging-in-Publication Data

deRubertis, Barbara.
Dilly Dog's dizzy dancing / by Barbara deRubertis ; illustrated by R.W. Alley.
p. cm. — (Animal Antics A to Z)
Summary: Teacher Alpha Betty demonstrates new ways of dancing to Dilly Dog so that
Dilly can continue to dance without creating mishaps.
ISBN 978-1-57565-307-5 (lib. bdg. : alk. paper) — ISBN 978-1-57565-303-7 (pbk. : alk. paper)
[1. Dogs—Fiction. 2. Dance—Fiction. 3. Animals—Fiction. 4. Alphabet—Fiction. 5.
Humorous stories.] I. Alley, R. W. (Robert W.), ill. II. Title.
PZ7.D4475Dl 2010
[E]—dc22   2009024485

10 9 8 7 6 5 4 3 2 1

First published in the United States of America in 2010 by Kane Press, Inc.
Printed in Hong Kong
Reinforced Library Binding by Muscle Bound Bindery, Minneapolis, MN

Series Editor: Juliana Hanford
Book Design: Edward Miller

Animal Antics A to Z is a trademark of Kane Press, Inc.

www.kanepress.com

Dilly was a dancing dog.
She loved doing her dizzy dances.

Some of her dancing was very daring.
And some was downright dangerous!

Dilly Dog's dizzy dancing led to
disaster after disaster.

The kids at Alpha Betty's school thought
Dilly was a little daffy.

They worried about Dilly!

At dawn one day, Dilly was doing her usual dizzy dancing.

She bounced on her bed as she did a wild dance.

Suddenly she hit the ceiling. BANG!

Then she hit the floor. THUD!

"DILLY!" called Daddy Dog.

"Come downstairs and see what
you've done!"

Dilly Dog felt dreadful when she
saw the disaster.

A flower pot was damaged.
Daffodils were dumped on the floor.

"I'm sorry, Daddy," said Dilly with dismay.
"My dancing was a little too dizzy."

"Oh, Dilly," Daddy replied.
"I know you adore your dizzy dancing.
But do TRY to be a bit more careful!"

The next day after school, Dilly danced down to the boat dock.

"She's a darling dog," whispered Dory Duck, who worked at the dock.

"But she's a tad dippy."

"She's definitely a dear," whispered Dory's helper, Danny.

"But she's a tad dotty."

13

Suddenly, Dilly decided to dance ON
the boat dock.

She was NOT wearing a life jacket.
And Dilly was dizzy from dancing.

She darted. She dipped.
She dove through the air.

"Be careful!" cried Dory and Danny together.

But Dilly Dog accidentally danced
right off the end of the dock.

The water was deep.
Dilly was in danger!

Without delay, Dory and Danny dove
down into the deep, dark water.

They dragged Dilly up, up, up.

Dilly dog-paddled back to the dock.

Dory and Danny duck-paddled beside her.

Daddy Dog came dashing down to the dock.

"Dilly! You're drenched!" said Daddy.
"And you could have drowned!"

"I'm sorry, Daddy," said Dilly with dismay.
"My dancing was definitely too dizzy."

"Dilly," said Daddy. "It makes me sad.
But I must ask you to stop dancing."

Then he bundled her up
and carried her home.

Dilly Dog was feeling dreadful when
she arrived at school the next day.

She told Alpha Betty about the
disaster on the bed.

She told Alpha Betty about the
disaster on the dock.

Dilly hung her head and cried.

"Daddy is disappointed in me.
My friends think I'm dopey.
I'm really down in the dumps."

Dilly's tears dripped on her dress.

"Don't be sad, Dilly!" said Alpha Betty.

"You are a dear little dog. You just need to learn to dance *differently*."

Then Alpha Betty said something
that dumbfounded Dilly Dog.

"Did you know that I used to be
a dancer?" Alpha Betty asked.

"No!" whispered Dilly.

"Yes!" said Alpha Betty.

"I can show you **delightful** dances!
Dreamy dances! DAZZLING dances!
Would you like to learn?"

"Oh, YES!" whispered Dilly.

Alpha Betty did some dance steps.

Dilly tried to do them, too.

Some of the steps were difficult.

Some were demanding.

But Dilly was determined.

Dilly Dog danced home that day.

But she danced differently than
she had ever danced before.

She waved to Dory and Danny Duck.

They called, "Hello, Dilly!
You're doing a dandy dance today!"

"Daddy! Look!" said Dilly
when she arrived home.

"I'm done with dizzy dancing!
Watch me dance NOW!"

29

Daddy was delighted with Dilly's new dance!

"Dilly!" he cried. "Your dance is *dazzling*!"

Her smile was dazzling, too.

And Dilly never had a dancing disaster again.

(Well, almost never!)

FUN FACTS

- Home: All over the world! Dogs are the oldest known animal pets.
- Family: There are more than 150 breeds of dogs, and they are in the same family as wolves and foxes. There are also millions of lovable mutts, like Dilly, who are a mixture of breeds!
- Size: Dogs come in every size and shape, from the tiny Chihuahua to the huge Great Dane.
- Favorite foods: Mostly meats and grains. And doggie biscuits!
- **Did You Know?** Dogs have amazing hearing and an awesome sense of smell—much better than humans!

LOOK BACK

Learning to identify letter sounds (phonemes) at the beginning, middle, and end of words is called "phonemic awareness."

- The word *dog* begins with the d sound. Listen to the words on page 30 being read again. When you hear a word that begins with the d sound, bark like a dog!
- The word *sad* ends with the d sound. Listen to the words on page 24 being read again. When you hear a word that ends with the d sound, quack like a duck!
- **Challenge**: The word *middle* has the d sound in the middle! Listen to the words on page 10 being read again. There is ONE word that begins with the d sound AND has the d sound in the middle. What is the word?

TRY THIS!

Dilly's Dizzy Dancing Game

Listen carefully as each word in the word bank is read aloud.

- If the word begins with the d sound, jump in the air!
- If the word ends with the d sound, sit down!
- If the word begins and ends with the d sound, spin around once!

dizzy bed dance
darted dock held
dress sad dear
delighted

FOR MORE ACTIVITIES, go to Dilly Dog's website: www.kanepress.com/AnimalAntics/DillyDog
You'll also find a recipe for Dilly Dog's Dilly Dip for Vegetables!

32

Dear Parent:
Your child's love of reading starts here!

Every child learns to read in a different way and at his or her own speed. You can help your young reader improve and become more confident by encouraging his or her own interests and abilities. You can also guide your child's spiritual development by reading stories with biblical values and Bible stories, like I Can Read! books published by Zonderkidz. From books your child reads with you to the first books he or she reads alone, there are I Can Read! books for every stage of reading:

SHARED READING
Basic language, word repetition, and whimsical illustrations, ideal for sharing with your emergent reader.

BEGINNING READING
Short sentences, familiar words, and simple concepts for children eager to read on their own.

READING WITH HELP
Engaging stories, longer sentences, and language play for developing readers.

READING ALONE
Complex plots, challenging vocabulary, and high-interest topics for the independent reader.

ADVANCED READING
Short paragraphs, chapters, and exciting themes for the perfect bridge to chapter books.

I Can Read! books have introduced children to the joy of reading since 1957. Featuring award-winning authors and illustrators and a fabulous cast of beloved characters, I Can Read! books set the standard for beginning readers.

A lifetime of discovery begins with the magical words *"I Can Read!"*

Visit www.icanread.com for information on enriching your child's reading experience.
Visit www.zonderkidz.com for more Zonderkidz I Can Read! titles.

"Rescue the weak and the needy."
—*Psalm 82:4*

ZONDERKIDZ

The Berenstain Bears'™ Kitten Rescue
Copyright © 2010 by Berenstain Publishing, Inc.
Illustrations © 2010 by Berenstain Publishing, Inc.

Requests for information should be addressed to:
Zonderkidz, *Grand Rapids, Michigan 49530*

Library of Congress Cataloging-in-Publication Data

Berenstain, Jan, 1923 –
    The Berenstain Bears' Kitten Rescue / written by Jan and Mike Berenstain.
       p.   cm. – (I can read. Level 1)
    ISBN 978-0310-72097-3 (softcover)
    [1. Cats—Fiction. 2. Animals—Infancy—Fiction. 3. Animal rescue—Fiction. 4. Bears—
    Fiction. 5. Christian life—Fiction.] I. Berenstain, Michael. II. The Berenstain Bears Kitten
    Rescue. III. Kitten rescue
    PZ7. B44826Bhk 2011
    [E]—dc22   2010016487

All Scripture quotations, unless otherwise indicated, are taken from the Holy Bible, *New International Version®, NIV®.* Copyright © 1973, 1978, 1984 by Biblica, Inc.™ Used by permission of Zondervan. All rights reserved worldwide.

Any Internet addresses (websites, blogs, etc.) and telephone numbers printed in this book are offered as a resource. They are not intended in any way to be or imply an endorsement by Zondervan, nor does Zondervan vouch for the content of these sites and numbers for the life of this book.

Editor: Mary Hassinger
Art direction & cover design: Jody Langley

Printed in China

10 11 12 13 14 15 /SCC/ 10 9 8 7 6 5 4 3 2 1

I Can Read!™ · BEGINNING READING 1

The Berenstain Bears'
KITTEN RESCUE

By Jan and Mike Berenstain

ZONDERVAN.com/
AUTHORTRACKER
follow your favorite authors

ZONDERkidz

"Are we ready for our good deed
of the day?" asked Scout Brother.
"What shall it be?" asked Scout Sister.
"How about ..." began Scout Fred.

"Wait a minute," said Scout Lizzy.

"I hear something."

There was a soft, "Mew! Mew!"

"Look!" said Lizzy.

"A kitten is stuck in that tree."

"We will get it down," said Brother.

"That will be our good deed!"

"As the Bible says," Fred pointed out,

"'Whoever is kind to the needy

honors God.'"

"Good point, Fred," said Brother.

"How will we get it down?" asked Lizzy.

"I will stand on your shoulders,"

said Brother.

Then Scouts Sister, Lizzy, and Fred

stood on each other's shoulders.

Brother climbed up.

But he lost his balance.

They all fell down!

"Now what?" asked Sister
from the bottom of the pile.
"We need a ladder," said Brother.
"Maybe Papa can help."

Brother and Sister ran home.

Papa Bear was glad to help.

They carried the ladder to the tree.

"I want you cubs safe," Papa said.

"You hold the ladder.

I'll climb up."

Papa climbed up the shaky ladder and

out on a branch.

When the kitten saw Papa,

it got scared. It climbed higher.

Papa could not reach it.

13

"We need help," said Papa.

"Brother and Sister, go get

the fire department."

"The fire department?" cried the scouts.

"Hooray!"

14

Brother and Sister ran to the firehouse.

They told the fire-bears about

the kitten up the tree.

The fire-bears sounded the alarm.

They put on their gear.

They climbed onto their fire truck.

Brother and Sister climbed on too.

Lights flashed! Sirens blew!

The fire truck roared across town!

The fire truck pulled up to the tree.
A crowd gathered to see what
was going on.

A news van came to take pictures.

The fire-bears raised their ladder

to reach the kitten.

The fire-bears climbed up.

But the lights and the siren

scared the kitten even more.

It climbed to the top of the tree.

Not even the fire-bears' long ladder

could reach the kitten.

A long, fancy car pulled up.

It was the mayor.

"What's going on?" he asked.

"It's a kitten up a tree, Mayor,"
said the fire chief.

"But we need help.

We need the rescue copter."

The fire chief got on his radio.

He called the rescue copter.

23

Soon, the copter flew in.

It lowered a rescue bear

on a long rope.

He tried to reach the kitten.

But the rescue copter scared it.

The kitten hid in the leaves.

Mama Bear came by with Honey Bear.

They were coming from the store.

"Mama!" said Sister.

"Did you get any cat food?"

"Yes," said Mama. "I got it for
our kitten, Gracie."

"May I have it, please?" Sister asked.

Sister opened the cat food.

"Here, kitty, kitty!" she called.

The kitten peeked out of the leaves.

"Mew?" it said.

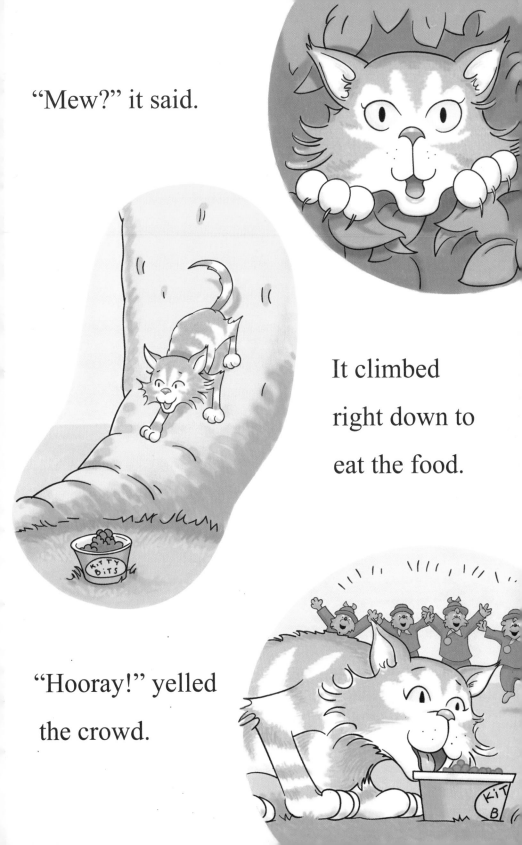

It climbed
right down to
eat the food.

"Hooray!" yelled
the crowd.

A lady ran out of the crowd.

"My kitten, Muffy!" she cried.

"Thank you so much

for saving her!

'I give thanks to the Lord, for he is good!'"

Everyone posed with the kitten.

The news bears took pictures.

Everyone was very proud

of the Good Deed Scouts.

Later, the Bear family watched the news.
They cheered when they
saw themselves on TV.
And they were very happy
that the kitten up a tree
was safe and sound.